The Fun Day Fairies

For Danielle Cropley,

with lots of love

Special thanks to

Narinder Dhami

ORCHARD BOOKS
338 Euston Road, London NW1 3BH
Orchard Books Australia
Hachette Children's Books
Level 17/207 Kent Street, Sydney, NSW 2000

A Paperback Original

First published in 2006 by Orchard Books
Rainbow Magic is a registered trademark of Working Partners Limited.
Series created by Working Partners Limited, London W6 OQT

Text © Working Partners Limited 2006
Illustrations © Georgie Ripper 2006

The right of Georgie Ripper to be identified as the illustrator of
this work has been asserted by her in accordance with the
Copyright, Designs and Patents Act, 1988.

A CIP catalogue record for this book is available from the British Library.

ISBN 978 1 84616 192 6

5 7 9 10 8 6

Printed in Great Britain

Orchard Books is a division of Hachette Children's Books

Freya
the Friday Fairy

by Daisy Meadows

illustrated by Georgie Ripper

ORCHARD BOOKS

www.rainbowmagic.co.uk

Icy wind now fiercely blow!
To the Time Tower I must go.
Goblin servants follow me
And steal the Fun Day Flags I need.

I know there will be no fun,
For fairies or humans once the flags are gone.
So, storm winds, take me where I say.
My plan for chaos starts today!

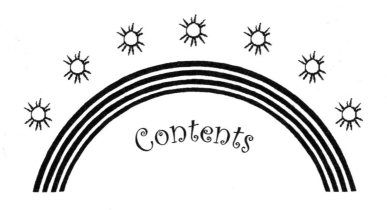

Contents

Cooking Up a Storm

"Here's the recipe, Kirsty," Rachel
Walker said, showing the cookery book
to her best friend Kirsty Tate. "Don't they
look yummy?"

Kirsty looked at the picture and nodded.
"I love gingerbread men!" she said.

"Gran always bakes gingerbread
men for my birthday," Rachel explained.

"So I thought we could make some for her as she's coming to tea today." She laughed as her shaggy dog Buttons trotted into the kitchen and looked up at the two girls hopefully. "Buttons likes them too!"

At that moment Mrs Walker, Rachel's mum, followed Buttons into the room.

"Gran will be here soon," she said. "We'd better get started, girls. I'll find the cookie cutter. You two collect the ingredients."

"OK, Mum," Rachel agreed. "I'll get the eggs. Kirsty, could you get the flour? It's in that cupboard near the sink."

Rachel opened the fridge and Kirsty went to find the flour. Meanwhile, Mrs Walker was searching through the drawers for the cookie cutter.

"Mum, we haven't got any eggs," Rachel called, her head still inside the fridge.

 "And there isn't any flour in the cupboard," added Kirsty, moving aside packets and boxes to check. "That's funny," Mrs Walker said, shaking her head. "I thought we had plenty of both. And I'm sure I saw the cookie cutter only a few days ago." She frowned. "Maybe it got taken up to the loft in that box of kitchen equipment we don't use any more. I'll go and check."

"We're not doing very well, are we?" Rachel sighed as her mum left the room. "This is no fun at all."

"You know why, don't you?" Kirsty pointed out. "It's because it's Friday, and Freya the Friday Fairy's flag is missing!"

Rachel and Kirsty shared a special, magical secret. They had become friends with the fairies, and were helping their tiny friends find the missing Fun Day Flags. Without the flags, the Fun Day Fairies couldn't recharge their wands with the wonderful magic that made every day of the week fun in the human world.

The flags had been stolen from Fairyland by nasty Jack Frost and his mean goblin servants. But Jack Frost had quickly become annoyed when the flags' magic meant that his goblins started having lots of fun and playing pranks, so he had cast a powerful spell to send the flags whirling away into the human world.

"You're right, Kirsty," Rachel agreed. "Oh, I hope we find Freya's flag today before the goblins do!"

The goblins had missed having fun so much that they'd sneaked off without Jack Frost's permission to get the flags back. But Rachel and Kirsty had managed to get the better of the goblins so far, and they'd already returned the Monday, Tuesday, Wednesday and Thursday flags to the fairies.

"We'll do our best," Kirsty replied firmly. "The Fun Day Fairies are depending on us."

Suddenly the doorbell rang. "That must be Gran!" Rachel exclaimed.

The two girls hurried down the

hall and Rachel opened the front door.
As she did so, a strong gust of wind
pushed the door open wide.

"Hello, girls," Gran said, smiling.
"I've had a lovely walk over here, but
isn't it windy?"

"Hi, Gran," Rachel replied, beaming as her gran gave her a big hug. "Come in."

"Hello," said Kirsty warmly.

"You must be Kirsty!" Gran declared, giving Kirsty a hug too.

"Do call me Gran, dear. I've heard so much about you, I feel like I know you already!" Kirsty smiled. "OK, Gran!" she agreed.

"It's very odd," Gran continued as she stepped into the hall. "While I was walking here, I had the strangest feeling that I was being followed – but when I looked there was nobody behind me." She laughed and shook her head. "I must be imagining things!"

Rachel closed the door as Gran unbuttoned her coat and hung it up in the cloakroom. As Gran turned back to the girls, Rachel noticed a beautiful lilac scarf knotted around her neck. The silky material looked familiar, and Rachel frowned.

"That's a pretty scarf, Gran," she said. "Have you worn it before?"

"No, I only bought it yesterday at a charity shop," Gran explained, untying the scarf. "I love the lilac colour and the sun pattern. Look!"

She shook the scarf out and held it up. Rachel and Kirsty glanced at each other in amazement.

It was the missing Fun Day Flag!

A Suspicious Salesman

"It's lovely, Gran," Rachel said.

"Yes, it is," Kirsty agreed. She winked at her friend as Gran tied the scarf back round her neck.

Just then Rachel's mum hurried down the stairs. "Hello, Mum," she said, kissing Gran on the cheek. Then she turned to Rachel and Kirsty.

"Sorry, girls, I couldn't find the cookie cutter in the loft. I'll have another look in the kitchen."

Rachel was so excited she could hardly wait until her mum and her gran had walked off to the kitchen out of earshot.

"Kirsty, we've already found the Friday flag!" she whispered, beaming all over her face. "I can hardly believe it!"

"You mean the flag found us," Kirsty pointed out. "What shall we do now? We can't take the scarf off your gran!"

Rachel thought for a moment.

"You're right, but the flag's quite safe for now," she replied. "We'll just have to wait for Freya to arrive."

"Meanwhile, we mustn't let the flag out of our sight," Kirsty said anxiously. "There may be goblins about."

Rachel nodded. Quickly the two girls hurried into the kitchen, where Gran was proudly showing the scarf to Mrs Walker.

"We were going to make gingerbread men for tea, Gran," Rachel explained. "But we couldn't find any flour or eggs."

"Or the cookie cutter," added Kirsty.

"Oh, well, Buttons needs a walk anyway," said Mrs Walker. "I'll take him out and pick up all the things we need at the same time."

"OK, Mum," replied Rachel. "Buttons! Walkies!" She took Buttons' lead off the hook by the back door and Buttons began jumping about excitedly, swishing his long furry tail. "I won't be long," Mrs Walker went on, picking up her coat. "Maybe you girls could get Gran a drink while I'm out."

"What would you like, Gran?" asked Rachel, as Mrs Walker and Buttons left the house.

"Oh, a glass of juice would be lovely, dear. Thank you," Gran replied.

While Gran went and sat down in the living room, Rachel and Kirsty got the juice out of the fridge.

"I wonder when Freya will get here," Kirsty said as they put the juice and three glasses on a tray.

"I'm sure she'll arrive before Gran goes home," replied Rachel. "If not, we'll have to think of a reason to borrow the scarf from Gran and take it back to Fairyland ourselves!"

Rachel carried the tray to the living-room and Kirsty went ahead to open the door for her. As Kirsty did so, she glanced over at the window and got the shock of her life! A mean, green face was staring at them through the glass. It was a goblin!

Rachel had put the tray down and was pouring Gran a glass of juice. She saw Kirsty staring at the window and looked over herself, catching a glimpse of the goblin just before he dodged out of sight. The girls glanced at each other anxiously.

"We're just going to tidy the kitchen, Gran," Rachel said breathlessly, and she and Kirsty hurried out into the hall.

"Your gran said she thought she was being followed – it must have been that goblin!" Kirsty whispered. "He's after the Fun Day Flag!"

"I wish Buttons was here," said Rachel, biting her lip. "The goblins are scared of dogs. He'd have kept them away."

"There could be more than one goblin too," said Kirsty. "What shall we do?"

But before they could decide, the doorbell rang. Both Kirsty and Rachel jumped. "It can't be Mum back already," Rachel said with a frown. "Anyway, she's probably taken her key. I wonder who it is?" The girls went down the hall and opened the front door cautiously. There on the doorstep was a very peculiar looking man. He was very short, but he was wearing an extremely long coat, as well as sunglasses and a big hat. He held a bunch of orange marigolds in his hand.

"I'm selling flowers," the man said in a rough, gruff voice. "Do you want some? They're very cheap!"

Rachel and Kirsty stared at the short
salesman. Kirsty could see a long green
nose poking out from under the hat,
and Rachel could see big, green feet
sticking out from under the hem
of the coat. The girls looked at each
other and nodded; the salesman was
a goblin!

"Look, lovely flowers!" the goblin said
impatiently, thrusting the flowers under
the girls' noses. Rachel
could see that some
of the flowers still
had roots attached
to the stems, and
she realised that
the goblin had just
torn them up from
the front garden!

"You'll buy them, won't you?" the goblin went on, hopping eagerly from one foot to the other. "All I want in return is one lilac scarf! Just one teeny-weeny little scarf, that's all! But it must be lilac, with a sun pattern on it!"

Rachel put her hands on her hips and stared hard at the goblin. "You're not fooling us for one minute, Mr Goblin!" she said firmly. "And my dad's going to be really annoyed that you've been pulling up his marigolds!"

The goblin scowled, threw the flowers at Kirsty and ran off down the path as fast as he could, almost tripping over the hem of his coat.

"I managed to catch most of the flowers!" Kirsty said, picking up one which had fallen on the step. "Maybe we can put them in a vase for your mum."

"We're going to have to protect Gran from the goblins!" Rachel said, closing the door.

Kirsty nodded. "I hope Freya gets here soon," she added.

At that moment, a burst of magical purple sparkles swirled from the bright orange marigolds in Kirsty's hand, and the next moment a tiny fairy popped her head out from between two of the flowers and waved at the girls.

"It's Freya the Friday Fairy," cried Rachel. "She's here!"

Goblins After Gran!

Freya fluttered out from the bunch
of flowers, lilac sparkles and orange
marigold petals drifting around her.
She wore a purple dress with long,
bell-shaped sleeves, a lilac belt with
a heart-shaped buckle and knee-length
purple boots.

"Hello, girls," Freya said eagerly.

"Do you know where the flag is? The Book of Days said you would."

The Book of Days was in Fairyland, looked after by Francis the Frog, the Royal Time Guard. Every morning he checked the book to make sure that he ran the correct Fun Day Flag up the flagpole on the Fairyland Time Tower. Since the flags had disappeared, poems had appeared in the Book of Days giving clues to their whereabouts.

Freya flicked back her curly blonde hair and recited:

"The girls will know its hiding place,
The trick will be to keep it safe,
Once the flag is in your care,
Beware the goblins everywhere!"

"Yes, we do know where the flag is, Freya," Kirsty said quickly.

"Hurrah!" Freya cried, twirling happily in mid-air. "I can't wait to see my beautiful flag again, but where is it?"

"It's round my gran's neck," Rachel explained. "She's wearing it as a scarf!"

"But there are goblins here too," added Kirsty. "We don't know how many."

Freya looked grave. "Girls, I think there could be lots of goblins! I saw two of them myself, hanging around by the back door."

"Oh, no!" Rachel gasped, looking worried. "That's where Buttons' dog flap is. The goblins are small enough to get into the house that way!"

Freya and Kirsty looked dismayed.

"Quick, we must find out if they're in the house!" Freya said urgently.

The girls rushed through the house to the back door with Freya zooming along behind. They reached it just in time to see two goblins creeping quietly into the living room.

"Gran's in there on her own!" whispered Rachel.

"With the flag," groaned Kirsty. "After them!"

Kirsty, Rachel and
Freya dashed to the
living room door.
Gran was sitting
on the sofa, just
finishing her juice,
and the goblins
were lurking behind
the back of the sofa,
whispering to each other
and pointing up at Gran.

Gran put down her empty glass and
reached for a magazine from the
coffee table. She sat back and began
flicking through the pages. Then,
before the girls could do anything, one
goblin climbed up onto the shoulders
of the other and slowly reached out to
pull the flag from around Gran's neck.

"Oh, no, you don't!" Rachel said loudly.

Gran looked startled and dropped the magazine. The goblins both jumped in fright and fell over, the top one tumbling off the shoulders of the other. Glaring at the girls, both goblins got to their feet and began dusting themselves down.

Freya landed on Kirsty's shoulder and hid behind her hair as the girls hurried into the room.

Meanwhile Gran was looking rather puzzled. "What's the matter, Rachel?" she asked. "Why don't you want me to read the magazine?"

"Er…um…" Rachel stammered, trying to think of something to say.

"Rachel just meant that she wanted to pass you the magazine," Kirsty said quickly. "She didn't want you to have to get up from the sofa."

Gran smiled. "I'm not so old that I can't get a magazine for myself," she laughed, as Rachel carefully gave the magazine back to her. "But thank you for being thoughtful."

As Gran flipped through the magazine, Rachel glanced over at the goblins. "I think we should get Gran out of the house," she whispered to Kirsty. "We have to keep her away from the goblins."

Kirsty nodded in agreement.

"Gran, would you like to come out and see the garden?" Rachel asked. "The flowers are lovely, and we bought a new birdbath last week."

"I'd love to, dear," Gran replied.

Rachel opened the French windows and they all went outside. Although it was still very windy, the patio was quite sheltered and it was lovely and warm in the sun.

"Remember to beware the goblins everywhere!" Freya whispered in Kirsty's ear.

Kirsty nodded to show she'd heard.

"There's the new birdbath, Gran," Rachel said, pointing to the middle of the lawn.

"It looks lovely," Gran said admiringly. "And aren't these marigolds beautiful?" she added, stopping to admire the bright orange flowers as they walked across the patio.

All of a sudden Kirsty caught a flash
of movement from the corner of her
eye. She looked round. Behind them
was the Walkers' washing line, which
ran the whole length of the garden.
A goblin was whizzing along the length
of it, hanging onto the line with his big
hands and sliding along! And he was
heading straight towards Gran, his
knobbly green fingers stretched out to
grab the Friday flag.

Disaster Strikes!

Rachel had also just spotted the goblin. She glanced at Kirsty, her eyes wide with dismay.

Kirsty knew they had to do something – and fast. "Oh, look!" she exclaimed loudly. "Is that a baby robin drinking from the birdbath?"

"Really?" Gran said, forgetting about the flowers and heading across the lawn towards the birdbath, just as the goblin sailed past and made a grab for the flag. He missed completely, and, unable to stop himself, whizzed to the end of the washing line and catapulted head first into a thick bush.

"I can't see the baby robin," Rachel said quickly. She could hear the goblin moaning and muttering behind her and she didn't want her gran to notice. "But isn't the birdbath lovely, Gran? Look at this engraved pattern on the side."

"And look at the beautiful dahlias at the bottom of the garden," Kirsty added helpfully.

Gran looked interested and the girls quickly led her away from the goblin.

"Well done," Freya whispered in Kirsty's ear.

"I just wonder how many more goblins are lurking about," Kirsty whispered back.

As they walked down the garden, away from the sheltered patio, the wind grew stronger. The big beech tree was swaying as they passed underneath it, and Rachel could see a long green branch hanging down.

The wind must have broken one of the branches, she thought. But then Rachel realised it wasn't a branch at all. It was a goblin hanging upside-down, waiting to grab the scarf!

His eyes were gleaming greedily as Gran got closer and closer. Rachel looked desperately over her shoulder at Kirsty and Freya, and pointed at the goblin. Immediately Freya popped out from behind Kirsty's hair and waved her wand. A few lilac sparkles whizzed towards Gran and drifted around the handbag she was carrying. Suddenly it fell from Gran's hand onto the path.

"Oh, dear!" Gran exclaimed. "How clumsy of me!" And she bent to pick up her bag at the very same time as the goblin made a grab for the flag. He missed and swung wildly to and fro, muttering crossly to himself. Then, glaring at Freya and the girls, he hoisted himself back up into the tree out of sight. Freya smiled and zoomed over to hide in Rachel's pocket.

"Thank you, Freya," Rachel said in a low voice while Kirsty pointed out the bright red dahlias to Gran.

"The flag isn't safe
while there are so
many goblins
around," said
Freya with
a frown. "We must
get it from your gran so that
I can take it safely back to Fairyland!"

Rachel nodded, an idea popping
into her head. "Gran, I really love
your new scarf," she said. "Could
I have another look at it, please?"

"Of course," Gran said, smiling.
She untied the scarf and held it
out to Rachel. But as she did so,
a strong gust of wind whipped it
out of her hand. Rachel reached
out for it but missed, and the flag
danced away from her on the breeze.

In another moment the wind had carried it away around the side of the house.

"Oh, no!" Gran exclaimed.

"We'll get it, Gran!" Rachel gasped. She and Kirsty ran off as fast as they could, with Freya still in Rachel's pocket, leaving Gran to look at the flowers.

"I can hear a goblin cackling," Kirsty groaned as they rushed round the side of the house and paused behind a large bush.

The girls and Freya peeped
around the bush.
A big goblin
was tying Gran's
scarf around
his neck, and
admiring his
reflection in the
glass of the side door.

"We're lucky your gran
can't see this side of the house from the
garden," Kirsty whispered.

Rachel nodded. "We have to get the
flag back!" she said softly. "But how?"

Time for a Trick

Freya and the girls watched the
goblin gleefully tying and untying
the scarf in lots of different ways.
He wound it round his head, like
a turban, then he knotted it like
a tie and then he put it around
his shoulders like a shawl, giggling
all the time.

"He's having loads of fun," Kirsty whispered. Then she caught her breath. "Oh!" she gasped. "That's given me an idea!"

"What?" Freya and Rachel asked.

"If we can fool the goblin into thinking that the flag isn't fun anymore, he won't want it!" Kirsty explained.

"Well, yes," Rachel agreed. "But how can we do that?"

Kirsty thought for a moment. "I bet the goblin wouldn't like it if he thought the flag was turning him purple!" she exclaimed, her eyes twinkling.

"You're right," Freya declared. "And I can change his reflection with my fairy magic." She laughed. "Come and watch the fun!" And, with that, Freya waved her wand, showering the girls in sparkling lilac fairy dust.

In the blink of an eye, the girls
became fairies with glittering wings
on their backs. They fluttered up into
the air to follow Freya, and the three
of them flew over to hover behind
the goblin.

He was now tying the scarf around
his head so that he looked like a pirate
and chuckling happily. Freya waved
her wand again, and Rachel and Kirsty
smiled as the goblin's
reflection in the
glass door turned
exactly the same
lilac colour
as the flag.

"Don't I look
handsome?" the
goblin said proudly,
admiring himself in
the glass. Then he peered more closely
at his reflection and gave a shriek
of horror. "I'm purple!" he yelled.
"Help! I've turned the same colour
as the flag!"

Freya and the girls hovered behind him, trying not to laugh out loud.

"I don't want to be purple," the goblin was groaning. "Goblins are green, not purple."

Freya tapped the goblin on the shoulder with her wand. "It's the flag," she said, pointing at his head. "The magic's not working properly."

Rachel laughed and pointed at the goblin. "You do look funny," she said. "I've never seen a purple goblin before!"

The goblin looked annoyed.

"Being purple isn't any fun, is it?" said Kirsty sympathetically.

"No, it isn't!" the goblin muttered, and he pulled the flag off his head and threw it down.

Immediately, Freya and the girls zoomed down to the flag. With a twirl of Freya's wand, the flag became its Fairyland size and Rachel scooped it up.

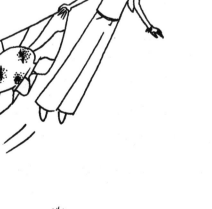

But just then the goblin glanced down at his arms, and his eyes almost popped out of his head. "I'm still green!" he gasped, looking from his arms to the glass door. "It's only my reflection that's

purple!" He began dancing up and down in a rage. "You tricked me!"

"We'd better get out of here," Freya said urgently, as the goblin rushed towards them, reaching for the flag.

Friday Fun!

At that moment, they all heard
a friendly bark.

"Woof! Woof!"

"That's Buttons!" Rachel cried, as
they also heard the front garden gate
open and close. "Mum's back!"

The goblin looked terrified. With
a squeal of terror, he dived head first

into a nearby lavender bush and disappeared. Kirsty, Rachel and Freya couldn't help laughing.

"I think we've probably seen the last of all the goblins now that Buttons is home," said Kirsty, grinning.

"Thank you so much, girls," Freya said gratefully as Rachel gave her the Friday flag. "Now I'll be able to take my flag back to Fairyland and recharge my Fun Day magic."

Rachel and Kirsty nodded happily. They knew that once Francis had run the Friday flag up the Time Tower flagpole, the sun's rays would strike the sparkly material. The rays would then be channelled directly down into the courtyard to charge Freya's wand with special magic so that she could make Fridays full of fun!

"Girls!" Rachel's mum called. "Where are you?"

"You'd better go," said Freya. "But before you do..." She twirled her wand and immediately an exact copy of the Friday flag appeared in Rachel's hand.

"It's for your gran," explained Freya.
"It's exactly the same as my flag, except
that it's not magic, of course! Now
goodbye, girls."

Rachel and Kirsty waved as the little
fairy vanished in a lilac mist of magic
dust. Then they hurried back into the
garden where Rachel's mum had joined
Gran. Buttons came running to meet them.

"Oh, you caught my scarf!" Gran declared happily. "Thank you, girls. It's so pretty, I wouldn't want to lose it." Gran tied the scarf firmly round her neck, and they all went inside.

"I bought some jelly beans and chocolate buttons to decorate the gingerbread men," said Mrs Walker, as they entered the kitchen "But I couldn't find a cookie cutter in the village shop. We'll just have to make gingerbread cakes instead."

But Rachel had just noticed a few lilac sparkles drifting around one of the kitchen drawers. Her heart pounding with excitement, she pulled it open.

Four sparkling silver cookie cutters lay in the drawer in front of her. One was in the shape of a fairy, one a castle, one a toadstool house and the fourth a winged horse. "Look at these!" Rachel said happily, placing them one by one on the kitchen worktop.

Kirsty's eyes opened wide. "Freya must have recharged her Fun Day Magic already!" she whispered, picking up the horse-shaped cookie cutter. "Look, Rachel, this is just like Pegasus. Do you remember meeting him when we found Lucy's magic Diamond?"

Rachel nodded. "Now we can have some fun!" she said with a smile.

Meanwhile Mrs Walker was looking bewildered. "I don't remember buying those," she said. "But aren't they lovely?"

"I'm looking forward to eating
a gingerbread fairy," Gran agreed
with a smile. "It'll make a change
from a boring old gingerbread man!"

Rachel beamed at Kirsty as they
began to mix the ingredients together.

"We can almost make a gingerbread Fairyland," she whispered, "thanks to Freya's Fun Day Magic!"

"And there are only two more Fun Day Flags to find before I go home on Sunday," said Kirsty. "I really hope we find them before the goblins do!"

RAINBOW magic ®

The Fun Day Fairies

Megan, Talullah, Willow, Thea and
Freya have got their flags back. Now
Rachel and Kirsty must help

Sienna the Saturday Fairy

Win Rainbow Magic goodies!

In every book in the Rainbow Magic Fun Day Fairies series (books 36–42) there is a hidden picture of a flag with a secret letter in it. Find all seven letters and re-arrange them to make a special Fairyland word, then send it to us. Each month we will put the entries into a draw and select one winner to receive a Rainbow Magic Sparkly T-shirt and Goody Bag!

Send your entry on a postcard to Rainbow Magic Fun Day Competition, Orchard Books, 338 Euston Road, London NW1 3BH. Australian readers should write to Hachette Children's Books, Level 17/207 Kent Street, Sydney, NSW 2000. New Zealand readers should write to Rainbow Magic Competition, 4 Whetu Place, Mairangi Bay, Auckland, NZ. Don't forget to include your name and address. Only one entry per child. Final draw: 30th September 2007.

Have you checked out the

website at:

www.rainbowmagic.co.uk

by Daisy Meadows

The Pet Keeper Fairies

The Fun Day Fairies

Coming soon:

Look out for the Petal Fairies!

TIA THE TULIP FAIRY
1-84616-457-5

PIPPA THE POPPY FAIRY
1-84616-458-3

LOUISE THE LILY FAIRY
1-84616-459-1

CHARLOTTE THE
SUNFLOWER FAIRY
1-84616-460-5

OLIVIA THE ORCHID FAIRY
1-84616-461-3

DANIELLE THE DAISY FAIRY
1-84616-462-1

ELLA THE ROSE FAIRY
1-84616-464-8